Katrin Hyman Tchana
AND
Louise Tchana Pami

ILLUSTRATED BY
Colin Bootman

SCHOLASTIC PRESS
New York

Library of Congress Cataloging-in-Publication Data

Tchana, Katrin.
Oh, no, Toto! / by Katrin Hyman Tchana and Louise Tchana Pami;
illustrated by Colin Bootman. p. cm.
Summary: Little Toto loves to eat, and when he goes with his grandmother
to the marketplace, he eats everything in sight, leaving chaos in his wake.
Includes a glossary of Cameroonian foods and a recipe for *egussi* soup.
ISBN 0-590-46585-6
[1. Food habits — Fiction. 2. Grandmothers — Fiction. 3. Cameroon — Fiction.]
I. Pami, Louise Tchana. II. Bootman, Colin, ill. III. Title.
PZ7. T21923Oh 1997 [E]—dc20
95-32075 CIP AC
12 11 10 9 8 7 6 5 4 3 2 1   7 8 9/9 0 1 2/0
Printed in the U.S.A.   36
First printing, April 1997

Book design by Marijka Kostiw

The text type was set in Korinna.
The display type was set in LaBamba.
The illustrations were rendered in oils.

*Special thanks to Jean-Pierre Enyegue,
Cameroon Mission to the United Nations,
for fact-checking the manuscript and the art.*

FOR

Dianne Hess

— K.H.T. AND L.T.P.

FOR

Eloria Mae Facey,
Wade A. Green Jr.,
Aaquil J. Bootman,
AND Karen Clarke

— C.B.

Toto Gourmand lives in Cameroon,

which is a beautiful country in West Africa. Toto got his name because he loves to eat all the time. When his mother and father and sisters and brothers and all the aunts and uncles and cousins saw how much he loved to eat, they called him Toto Gourmand, which means Toto, the Hungry One.

One day, Big Mami said to Toto, "Tonight your Aunt Esther and Uncle John are coming for dinner. I'm going to market to buy some meat and yams, so we can cook them *egussi* soup. You may come, too, Toto, but you must behave yourself." Toto was very happy to go to market with his grandmother, and he promised to behave.

There were so many people in the market! Toto held on tightly to Big Mami's *wrappa* so that he wouldn't get lost. But soon he saw the puffpuff girl cooking puffpuffs in a big pot of hot cil. They looked so delicious!

"Big Mami, Big Mami!" Toto pulled at his grandmother's hand and pointed right at the puffpuffs.

"Toto Gourmand, you are always hungry," Big Mami said. "But you may have one puffpuff."

Before Big Mami could blink an eye, Toto was off.

He looked at the pile of puffpuffs. Which one should he choose? There was one at the bottom of the pile that looked bigger and better than the rest. Toto reached out to take it. But as he did, the others fell onto the sand.

"*Oh, no, Toto!*" the puffpuff girl said as Toto began to gobble up all the ones he'd spilled.

"*Waaah!*" cried Big Mami when she saw what Toto had done. "What am I going to do with you?" But Toto was too little to know any better. So Big Mami paid the puffpuff girl for the puff-puffs Toto had spilled. And off they went through the market to buy some meat.

While Big Mami bought some meat, Toto noticed the egg boy selling hard-boiled eggs. He carried them on a tray on top of his head. They looked so delicious! Eggs with salt and hot pepper! That made Toto very hungry. He climbed up onto the top of the stall. When the egg boy passed below him, Toto reached out and took one of the eggs off the tray and began to eat it right away.

"Oh, no, Toto!" the egg boy cried.

He knew at once what had happened.

Quicker than lightning, the egg boy put
his tray on the ground and caught Toto up by
the legs.

"*Waaah!*" cried Big Mami when she saw
that Toto was upside down. "What am I going
to do with you?"

But she knew that Toto was too little to
know better. So she paid the egg boy for Toto's
egg, and off they went through the market to
buy some oil.

Big Mami picked up her basket and pushed quickly between the rows of tables piled high with vegetables, groundnuts, red beans, dried fish, cassava sticks, and every sort of food you can imagine, to where the men were selling palm oil.

"Hey, Mami, Mami, come buy your oil here. I have the best oil for you!" the palm oil sellers called out. But Big Mami went straight to her friend Pa Walter.

Before anyone could stop him, Toto saw Pa Walter's pet monkey sitting on top of the barrel of palm oil, eating a banana. That banana looked so delicious! It made Toto very hungry. He climbed up next to the monkey and tried to grab the banana.

"Oh, no, Toto!" cried Pa Walter.

But it was too late.

The monkey quickly moved away, and...

...*S P L A S H !*

Toto fell right into the middle of Pa Walter's tub of palm oil.

"*Waaah!*" cried Big Mami. "What am I going to do with you?"

Big Mami looked at Toto and shook her head sadly. "Oh, Toto, you have ruined all of your clothes and now you are all wet and slippery and red. We'll have to go home right away, and I haven't even finished my shopping."

Big Mami hurried through the marketplace, and Toto hung on to her *wrappa* with his greasy hands. He did his best to follow quickly.

Then Big Mami saw Mami Peter sitting at a table selling garlic, ginger, yams, and *egussi*, and eating a plate of *koki* with a cassava stick.

"Mami Peter! How now?" Big Mami went to greet her friend.

"Heeey, what has happened to little Toto Gourmand?" cried Mami Peter in amazement. "Why is he covered with palm oil? What has he gotten into this time?"

"Oh, my friend, I don't know where to begin. Thank goodness I saw you, because I was just about to go home without half the things I need."

As Mami Peter showed Big Mami her best yams and *egussi*, Toto noticed the plate of *koki* with the cassava stick that Mami Peter had put on the ground under her table. It looked so delicious! He quietly lay down on his belly and wriggled under the table to get closer to the plate. He took a little bite of *koki*. *Mmmm!* It tasted so good. He took another bite. And another. Soon it was all gone. Then he ate the cassava stick, too.

When Big Mami finished her shopping, she put the *egussi* in her basket and the yams on her head. "Toto, Toto, where are you now?" she called.

When Toto heard Big Mami call his name, he crawled out from under the table.

"*Oh, no, Toto!* Just look at you!" Big Mami cried in dismay. "All your clothes are covered in sand! What were you doing under the table?"

"You ask what he was doing?" exclaimed Mami Peter, holding up her empty plate. "That child has eaten all of my *koki*, and my cassava stick, too! Take him home right away, Big Mami, before he eats up everything in the market!"

Big Mami didn't have enough money for Toto to eat *everything* in the market, so she agreed with Mami Peter. It was time to take Toto home.

When Toto and Big Mami got home, Uncle John and Aunt Esther were there. Big Mami told them the story of Toto Gourmand in the market.

"Waaah!" cried Aunt Esther when she saw Toto all covered with oil and sand. Then she took Toto to the bedroom and changed his clothes. "Now you stay away from the kitchen and don't eat another thing until we call you," she reminded him.

Toto stayed in the bedroom and played by himself. But after a while, a wonderful smell floated into his room. It smelled so good, he forgot he was supposed to stay away until he was called for dinner. *What could it be?* He followed it into the kitchen.

A big pot on the kitchen floor caught Toto's eye. *Mmmmm!* he thought. *This is what I've been looking for!* The pot was full of tender meat and tasty *egussi* soup. Toto sat down next to the pot. First he ate up all the meat. Then he drank up all the soup, until the pot was empty and his belly was full.

What delicious soup it was! What a wonderful day it had been! But now Toto was sleepy. *If only Big Mami would take me to the market every day*, he thought as he curled up next to the empty soup pot and fell fast asleep....

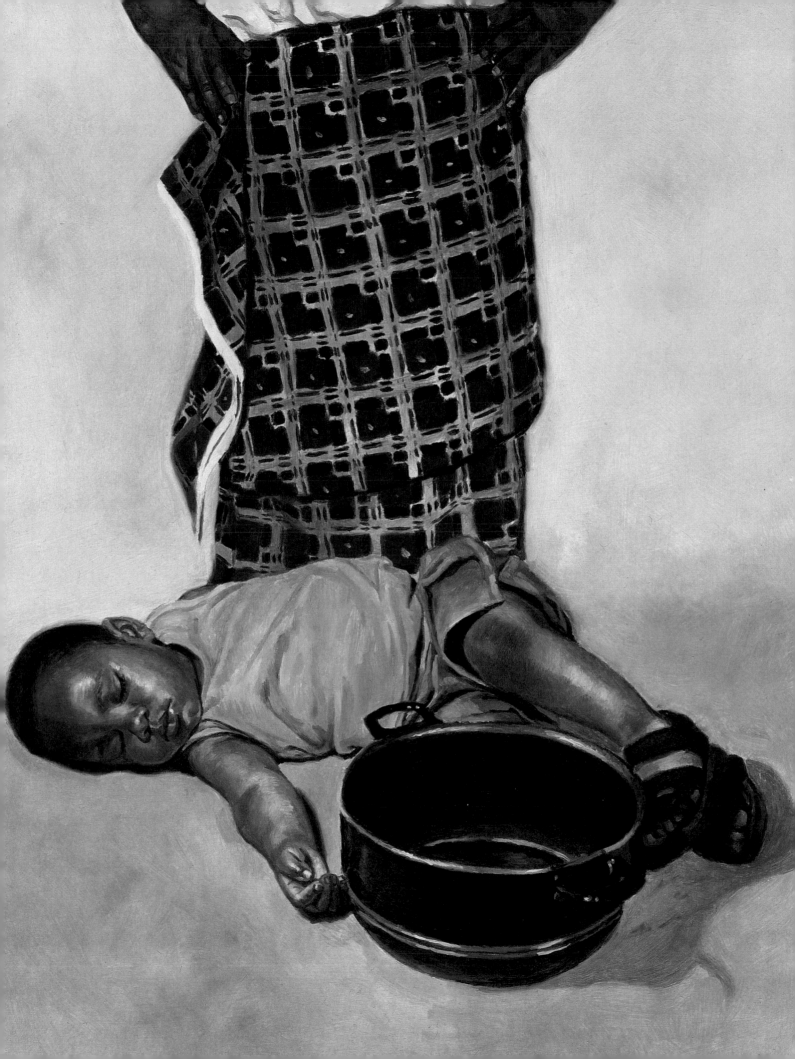

Author's Note

There are over 250 native languages spoken in the Republic of Cameroon, but French and English are the official languages used in the schools and by the government.

Louise Tchana Pami was brought up in Francophone Cameroon, where her primary language was French. Louise and I first wrote this story in French and then translated it into English. In the translation, we used many words and expressions that are specific to Cameroonian Pidgin English, the form of English that is widely spoken in the marketplace. For example, "How now?" is a common greeting in English-speaking Cameroon for "How are you?" And "Big Mami" is a name for "Grandma."

Toto's name, which is the French nickname for Thomas, was inspired by a primary school textbook that was widely used in French-speaking Africa in the 1950s and 1960s. Toto was a character who was always eating. Today "Toto" is used as an affectionate name for any young child who loves food.

—K.H.T.

Glossary of Cameroonian Foods in This Story

Cassava (cah • SAH • vah) **sticks**: Cassava is a root that is also used for making tapioca. Cassava sticks are made from fermented cassava, which is crushed and wrapped in banana leaves, then boiled. They have the same consistency as hard Jell-O.

Egussi (egg • OO • see) **seeds**: These seeds come from a kind of squash and taste a lot like pumpkin seeds, but they are white. They are crushed into a paste to make *egussi* soup.

Egussi (egg • OO • see) **soup**: A thick, spicy stew made of meat, vegetables, herbs, and spices. (The recipe is on the back cover of this book!)

Hot pepper: The hot pepper that Toto eats with his egg is a Scotch bonnet pepper. Scotch bonnet peppers are so hot that your hands burn when you touch them.

Koki (ko • KEE): This is a delicious dish made from mashed beans or corn, hot pepper, salt, and palm oil. It can be baked in a coffee can or steamed in banana leaves.

Palm oil: This is made from pressing palm nuts, the nuts that grow on palm trees. It is red and very heavy, and it has a strong flavor.

Puffpuffs: These balls of dough are like a doughnut without the hole, but they are not sweet. They are a popular breakfast food in Cameroon, especially when eaten with very hot red beans.

Yams: The yams Big Mami bought are not like sweet potatoes. They are very big roots, which are sold in sections as big as a man's upper arm! Inside they are pure white, and they taste a little bit like white potatoes, but are much drier.

Other Books Set in Cameroon

Alexander, Lloyd. *The Fortune-tellers*. Illustrated by Trina Schart Hyman. New York: Dutton, 1992.

Grifalconi, Ann. *The Village of Round and Square Houses*. Boston: Little, Brown and Company, 1986.